December

Snow

By Mercedes Guy Moore

Intro

When her father passed away from a heart attack, she had everyone around her fooled. Poor December. Lost both of her real parents. How devastating. . . I knew better.

I married her father not long after her mother was killed. I had been in love with Miles since I first heard him sing during tryouts for Midsummer Nights: The Musical, our high school's production. He had the tough, sexy guy look, like Daughtry, but a smooth, dreamy voice, like Michael Bublé. I had seen him around school before then, of course, and I always thought he had that classic, attractive look with his slick black hair, piercing crystal blue eyes, and standard leather jacket with a jersey hood. When I heard him sing, however, it was instant love.

I worked stage crew, so our paths would often cross. As we spent more time working on the play together, we got to know one another and became friends. Good friends. But every intimate moment we almost shared was overshadowed by his female lead counterpart, Frostine. Frost was the object of every male student's attention. Miles was not immune to Frost's sly, icy blue-gray eyes, beautiful snow-white skin, and long locks of fiery red hair. It didn't matter how close I tried to get to Miles, him and Frost were closer. By the end of the musical, the two were inseparable, and I was iced out. They got engaged senior year in front of the whole class at the Winter Wonderland Prom, after being announced as the Winter King and Queen. They were married right out of high school and Frost announced her pregnancy that following Fall.

It was not until our ten-year high school reunion that we reconnected. To say Frost did not care about us rekindling our friendship would have been an understatement. Frost barely even paid attention to her husband the entire night. She was too busy bragging about her perfect life to her old lackeys while Miles spilled how imperfect their life truly was. It was that night he confessed to me that he wished he had waited instead of getting married right out of school. "She has a way of making anything sound like a great idea," he said, sighing into his cake vodka spiked punch. "If she had asked me to jump off a cliff, I probably would have." He snorted at the thought.

It killed me to see him feeling so low. Ten years later and my feelings for him hadn't changed. If anything, my love for him only grew that night. I knew it was foolish to love a married man. Even though he was unhappy with Frost, his daughter, December, was his world. Knowing him the way I always had, he would do whatever it took to keep his family together.

Sitting across from him that night, it felt like we were back in high school, for real. His black hair was slicked back, his eyes were still piercing blue, with a small ring of darkness around them from age and being overworked. His tired eyes stared deep into his cup, lost in his sea of mistakes. I took his hand in mine as an attempt to comfort him. His hands were rough from all his years working on machine maintenance at the factory he was finally running. His eyes met mine and his raspberry colored lips curved up into a half-moon smile. "Your hands are warm," he had said. "Hers are always so cold."

We kept in touch after that night and talked almost every day and met for lunch once a week. While nothing ever passed the boundary of friendship, I was beginning to feel guilty for spending so much time with a married man. When I brought it up one day at lunch, he assured me, a little sadly, that Frost didn't even notice.

November

It was another handful of years later when Frost was murdered. She was found at a cabin on the other side of town, in the snow, with her heart cut out.

Miles showed up on my doorstep immediately after the police had visited his house. I didn't know the proper way to comfort a married man who I was hopelessly in love with after his wife was murdered. "Yay!" seemed a little insensitive. I reached out to take his hand in mine. He grabbed my hand and used it to pull me into his arms. I flew into his broad chest, breathing in his cologne that smelled like summer wind. His embrace was warm, comforting, and everything I ever thought it would be.

Miles was taller than me, so my head fit perfectly under his chin. His warm breath felt like sunshine warming my scalp. He sighed into my hair. "I don't know how to feel," he confessed. "Mostly, I just feel numb."

After soaking up most of his embrace, I invited him inside. It was his first time being in my apartment, but he made himself at home. He stepped through the doorway, slipping right out of his old, scuffed up work shoes, dragging his feet into the living room, and slumped into the worn-out couch.

I suddenly felt very self-conscious about the conditions of my apartment. It wasn't dirty, necessarily, but most of my furniture was torn up and ratty from my cats' kitten days. I had two Siamese cats, sisters. Mew, the out-going one, immediately took a liking to Miles. Mew hopped right onto his lap, kneading his legs before deciding he was suitable. She curled up in a ball on his legs, purring up a storm. Miles hardly even notice she was there as he mindlessly began to pet her.

Behind the couch, was the half-wall separating the living room and the kitchen. I stepped into the kitchen to start a pot of tea. As the kettle began to heat up, I started to get Miles' cup ready. I grabbed an orange flavored tea bag, two small spoonfuls of sugar and just a splash of whole milk so it tasted like a creamsicle. The kettle began to squeal and I removed it from the burner to fill up his mug. After giving it a quick stir, I brought the steaming beverage to Miles.

He clasped the mug in his hands, inhaling the vapors with a sigh. After taking a few more deep breaths, Miles took a long sip of his tea. He let out another sigh. "You always know exactly what I need." After a beat, he added, "Almost eighteen years together and it was like she knew nothing about me. It was as if she didn't care to know anything about me. . ." He took another long sip.

I didn't know how to respond. What was the appropriate thing to say for someone in my position?

Staring deep into his mug, he let out another confession. "I should be devastated. At the very least, upset. Instead, I feel. . ." He let out something between a huff and a laugh. "relieved."

I sucked in my breath. Again, at a loss for words.

Miles didn't seem to notice. He carried on the conversation for the both of us. "December is completely at a loss. She and her mother were so close. . . I don't know what I can do to help her get through this."

He was quiet for a moment. I took that moment to awkwardly sip my own tea; chamomile, no sugar.

"She's staying with her mom's sister, January, for a while."

"That's good," I replied, realizing it was the first thing I had said since he came in.

He nodded in agreeance. For a while, we just sat in silence. Mew was quietly asleep on Miles' lap. Nina was peering around the wall from the hallway, watching us, too afraid to join. I only looked at her from the corner of my eye, knowing that if I looked at her directly, she would flee.

After minutes had silently ticked away, he sadly stated, "I should probably be getting home."

"Oh. . . Okay."

He remained seated, his eyes still focused on his mug. "I'm not completely comfortable being in the house alone."

"That's understandable," I thought out loud.

"I was hoping you would understand." He half smiled.

He was too far away for me to hold his hand or place my hand on his shoulder, or leg. It felt like the physical distance between us was growing. Soon, he would go home. If he left, I knew it would be a long while before I saw him again. He had a lot to have to sort out. That would mean the end of our weekly lunch dates. I knew I was being selfish, worrying about such trivial things after what had happened to Frost. To Miles and his daughter. I knew it was wrong, but I couldn't help but wonder what Frostine's death would mean for Miles and me.

I was so deep in my own thoughts, I didn't hear Miles when he asked if I would stay at his house. "Lana, did you hear me?"

"I'm sorry. What did you ask?"

"Will you stay at the house with me for a while? Just while December is at her aunt's?"

I could feel my entire face flame up. Miles and I, sleeping under one roof? "Oh. Yeah. Yeah. Whatever you need."

Miles waited as I packed my suitcase. I was so flustered that I just grabbed whatever I could get my hands on. That meant my entire clean laundry basket and everything that was visible on my bathroom vanity and in the shower.

Miles went into his Lincoln Continental and I followed behind him in my '97 Jeep. I knew Miles was well off, but as I followed him into the gated community, I realized I did not know exactly how well off he actually was. We pulled up to his house and I tried hard not to faint behind the wheel. His steps were stone. The fencing around the porch was black wrought iron with swirly S's between each post. The house reminded me of where a witch would live in a bad made-for-TV movie. There was a long stone chimney on the back left-hand side of the house and the entire home itself was black, except for the gutters and shutters of the windows, which were a cream color. The windows were lavishly large and equally inviting and intimidating. I suddenly felt very small. I knew Miles worked his ass off to afford the house, but it was so clearly and painfully picked out by Frostine. Every small detail screamed her name.

I used both hands to pull my heavy suitcase up the steps to the front porch. "It's beautiful," I breathed, still taking it all in. I was staring up at the balcony on the front left-hand side of the house, figuring it was part of the master bedroom. I was close. The balcony in the front of the house belonged to December and the master bedroom was also on the second floor, but in the back of the house. I walked in and immediately had to lift my jaw from the cherry wood floor. A canopy draped down over the bed, flecks of gold shimmering from the incoming light of the balcony. The rustic metal head frame of the California King-sized bed was pressed up against the dark gray wall, facing the stone fireplace. Opposite from where we stood at the entrance, were the set of sliding glass doors, perfectly framing the view of the large pond in their backyard. Mindlessly, I found myself walking toward the balcony. Not daring to smudge the glass with my fingertips, they hovered over the glass as I peered out. Large Oak trees circled around the pond, their thick brown trunks forming a natural wall around it. Burnt orange and rusted red leaves sprinkled down, dusting the ground.

"In the winter, when it ices over, Frost and December use the pond as an ice-rink. It always seemed like there was no other place those two belonged but on the ice, their cheeks and noses rosy from the brisk air."

He stared out past me and at the pond, lost in his fond memories of his family. I felt as if I was intruding where I didn't belong. "I'm sorry."

Miles looked down at me, his crystal eyes glistening and he squeezed my shoulder. Changing the subject, he gestured out to the room with his left hand, his right hand still on my shoulder. "This is all yours."

"Oh, no." I immediately objected and shook my head. He wanted me to stay in the room he shared with his wife? In their bed? "I couldn't."

"I insist. It's the best room in the house! I will sleep downstairs in the guest room."

I felt guilty, like me being there was putting him out. Still shaking my head, I started, "Miles. . ."

"I just can't do it. Stay in here."

I nodded, understanding.

Miles continued, "The bed is brand new. She insisted that she wouldn't be able to sleep another night without it. It's one of those ghost beds. They're supposed to be the best or something, I don't know. All I know is it didn't break the bank and that was really all I cared about. . ." He paused to take a breath. "Anyway, it hasn't even been used yet. It just came in today. I thought I would surprise her."

I nodded my head again. Since there was no other response I could think of that would be sufficient, I set my suitcase down in front of the bed and pressed the retractable handle down so he knew I was accepting his offer to take the master bedroom.

His shoulders sagged with relief. For a few irreplaceable moments, we didn't say a word. We simply looked into each other's eyes with a slight smile mirrored on both of our faces.

*

I built a fire in the fireplace that night before bed. I propped up the pillows so I could sit up and lean against them while I finished The Great Gatsby for the millionth time. The chandelier above the bed clung to the ceiling with its roots, the trunk reached down and the branches extended out, small fairy lights budding off the branches like leaves. With the lights off and the flames licking the logs in the fire, the lights reaching off the branches of the chandelier looked more like twinkling icicles. I didn't know if it was the ghost bed, or the lullaby of the wood crackling and popping as the flames chewed into their bark, but I had fallen asleep before I even got to the part where Daisy hit Myrtle with Gatsby's car.

It was not until there was nothing left but ashes and memories of flames when I awoke in the dark room. I was expecting to find my book sprawled open on my lap. Instead, Miles' arm was resting on my stomach and my book was marked with a tissue on the bed stand next to me. Careful not to disturb Miles, I slid down into a laying position. Despite my heart fluttering in my throat, I fell back to sleep.

That was how it went for the rest of the week. Each night, Miles and I would go to sleep in our separate rooms and, in the middle of the night, he would slip into bed next to me. He just couldn't sleep alone, he said. I didn't mind. It was a dream to sleep next to him each night and wake up to his handsome face each morning. I would lay next to him, not daring to wake him up, and soak him in. I was memorizing his face, finding new things each morning, like the thin wrinkles extending out from the corners of his eyes like wings.

Miles was constantly moving. With work, meeting with the investigators who were looking into Frostine's death, and trying to plan her funeral before winter came and the ground was too cold to bury her, the precious and quiet moments where he did not have anything to do or to stress about were few and far between. All I knew was I got to be a part of those moments and that made me happy.

I did not go to the funeral. If I felt guilty about staying with Miles and sleeping in the same bed as him every night, then me going to his wife's funeral would definitely be inappropriate. December was supposed to come home with him afterwards, so I packed up my things so I could give them some space as a family. I, of course, waited until the last minute to get started. I wasn't ready to wake up from the dream yet.

Just as I was on my way down the iron, spiral staircase, my suitcase grating against each step behind me, Miles called. "Don't leave," he breathed before I could even say hello. "December wants to stay with her aunt a while longer."

"I'll be here." I dragged my suitcase back up the steps and into what I was tempted to start calling *our* bedroom.

December

His daughter stayed with her aunt for the entirety of November and the first week of December. It was at that point she decided to come home. Once Miles received her coming home call, I had already mentally prepared myself to leave and return to my one-bedroom apartment with my two cats. I stood before the sky blue, vintage style dresser, opened the top drawer and started to take my clothes out when Miles put his hand over mine and asked, "Where are you going?"

"Home."

Miles cupped my chin with his calloused hands so I was looking into his eyes. "I thought I made it clear. You are home."

With his cool eyes looking down at me, my cheeks were ablaze under his deep gaze. No matter how I struggled to keep my eyes from watering, I couldn't blink or look away. I knew all I was to him was a source of comfort, that he was using me for his own emotional needs. I also knew he was unaware that was what this was. All he knew was that he needed me. That was enough.

A couple of tears finally fled from behind my eyelids as his tough lips melted into mine. I sighed into his mouth with relief and excitement. My heart felt like a balloon about to burst as our tongues met. Miles pulled me away from the dresser and I fell onto the bed with a gasp. He leaned over me, brushing my auburn hair off my face and looking so deep into my eyes, I felt as though he was reading into my soul. I was about to ask him if he was sure this was what he wanted, when he hushed my lips with his. Tangled together and gasping for air, we united as one burning flame.

*

December's hair was jet black like her father's and her skin was snow white like her mother's. The contrast only made her that bit more beautiful. Her stunning blue eyes looked right through me when we first met. I felt like I was back in high school, eager to get approval from the gorgeous popular kids, but ended up invisible to them. She didn't even acknowledge I was there until her father introduced me. Even then, when she smiled it was empty. I knew not to take it personally. I was some strange woman who started living in their home right after her mother passed away. If I was her, I would hate me.

That was the thing though, she never acted like she hated me. Often, I wondered if she had any emotions at all. Everything she said, everything she did, was well thought out. She never said or did anything on impulse or blinded with passion.

Miles couldn't see it. She was his daughter after all. His snow angel. Nothing could be off about her…

We let the rest of the month of December serve as a trial before I officially moved in. I did not have a lot. I sold all my furniture and donated most of my kitchen supplies, no longer seeing the need to keep any of it since Miles' stuff was so much nicer than mine. As all my clothes and toiletries were already at his house, all I really had left to bring were some books, a couple of miscellaneous knick-knacks, and of course, my two cats.

I set them free in their new home just as December was stepping into the living room where I set up their toys. Nina, predictably, scampered off into the other direction. Mew sauntered right up to December and I smiled, expecting her to rub up against her jeans. Mew and December made eye contact. All I could think was, in that moment, Mew saw into December's heart and saw something dark. Perhaps nothing at all. For the first time ever, I heard Mew begin to hiss and watched in awe as she arched her back, her tail fluffed, and she slowly backed away.
December scowled and rolled her eyes. To herself, but loud enough for me to hear, she mumbled, "He had to pick the cat lady."

Mostly, I tried to write off her peculiar, sometimes troubling behavior. It wasn't fair of me to expect that she would welcome me or my cats with open arms. Maybe she wasn't a cat person, I tried to reason with myself. Not everyone liked cats and that was fine. I could accept that.

April

Miles proposed to me in the Spring. He took December and me to a small local theatre where they were producing an original musical. December and I took our seats while Miles ran off to use the restroom. He was gone for a long time, leaving December and I to sit next to each other in a painful silence.

The curtains were opening and he still hadn't come back. "I wonder where he is?"

December shrugged.

"Maybe I should go look for him." I had my hands on the arm rests about to stand myself up when I heard his voice. He stood on stage and began to sing. His voice was just as enchanting as it was the first time I heard it. Without music to accompany him, his voice soared through the theatre as he sang words of love. Of all the faces in the crowd, his alluring blue eyes found mine. Everyone else faded away until it was just him and me. As the song trailed to an end, he began to apologize. "I'm sorry everyone. This is not part of the show, but there is a woman in this audience who I need to ask a question to."

My heart flew into my throat and beat erratically against the walls of my esophagus.

"She has been my best friend for too many years to count. Other people may think this is too soon, but I know I have loved her for a long time already. Lately, she has been there every time I needed her and always knows how to take care of me. Lana, will you come up here?"

For a moment, I was frozen. I was dreaming. I knew I had to be dreaming because Miles was standing on a stage saying everything I have ever fantasized he would say, in front of a crowd of people.

December pushed me and snapped me out of it. "Go."

I didn't even feel my legs as I made my way down the aisle. I was numb until Miles took my hand in his to pull me up stage and pulses of electricity zapped through my palm and flew up my arm. I watched in disbelief as Miles knelt on one knee. He pulled a small box from his slacks, lifting the lid to reveal the ring. He said, "You have taken care of me. Now let me take care of you. Will you marry me?"

The simplicity of the ring made me smile. There was a single square cut diamond sparkling up at me from its placement in the thin gold band. It was perfect.

"Yes."

Everyone in the audience stood up as they clapped their hands. The spotlights on us twinkled like stars. Miles slipped the ring on my finger where it rested snuggly. He took my face in his cool, rough hands, and kissed me in front of the entire crowd. My heart was so full of bliss, I felt like we were floating. He pulled his lips away, resting his forehead on mine and stroking my cheek with his thumb. "I have always loved you," I whispered.

"I know."

The real show had to go on, of course. I went back to my seat, floating, completely belated. I watched my fiancé perform, oblivious to the ice-cold glares being shot at me by December.

July

We were married that summer. Most woman will attest to how stressful wedding planning is, especially planning a wedding in such little time, but I was a simple woman, as Miles knew. All I needed was him at my side and nothing more. That was why we got married in the park, under a large willow. Just Miles, me, and December. We had a friend play photographer and found someone to perform the ceremony instead of a priest because neither of us were really religious. It was perfect. Just as every moment with Miles had been.

Of course, now I look back wondering if things would have ended differently if a man of faith had blessed our marriage. Maybe then Miles would still be alive.

*

We didn't do anything too crazy for our honeymoon. There was only ever one place I wanted to see, the Apostle Islands in Wisconsin. That was where my parents went on their honeymoon, and I had vowed that if ever there came a day, that is where I would go as well. We camped on Stockton Island, right on the water and rented a double kayak for the duration of our trip. Our nights were spent warming each other by the fire and making love under the trees and stars. The days were filled with kayaking on Lake Superior and exploring the other islands. Especially those off limits. The best was probably swimming under the sea caves at Devils Island. The water was so blue under the clear sky that it twinkled. The caves were formed with a natural rock structure that almost looked like clay.

We beached our kayaks and swam where we couldn't be seen. Miles' wet, jet black hair was slicked back and the water made his pecks glisten. My fingertips traced the outline of his abs as I lost myself in his crystal blue eyes, like I always did.

His raspberry colored lips curved into his boyish grin. He shined.

Tracing my jawline with his calloused fingers sent waves of desire down my body. "You're so beautiful," he breathed.

I wanted to tell him he was wrong. That I was nothing compared to him. Compared to Frost. But he silenced me with one of his fervent kisses as he took ahold of my thigh and lifted my legs around him. In the cool water, our passion boiled.

*

December stayed home to take care of the cats for me. When we came back, I expected Mew to rush to the front door meowing for attention from her mother who had been away for a week. When we came home, however, she didn't come to the door. I searched all over that damn house and all I could find was her sister, Nina, who was closed in the linen closet. She was howling until I found her and set her free. Even then, she leapt into my arms and continued to cry. I knew I was only gone a week, but she had significantly lost weight to the point where her ribs were starting to show beneath her fur. "How long have you been in there?" Her body vibrated against my chest as she purred, rubbing her face against mine. I buried my nose into her soft fur. "Where is your sister?"

Miles stood beside me. "Oh, you found her?"

"This is Nina." I looked him in the eyes so he could see how upset I was. "She was in the closet the whole week."

Without missing a beat, he put his arm around my waist and said, "I'm sure it wasn't on purpose."

I did not believe that, but I let the topic drop. I attempted to bring Nina down stairs to her food and water dishes, but when Nina saw where December was leaning against the stairwell, she immediately started to squirm in my arms until she escaped my grasp. She darted from my hands, landing on all fours, and dashed into my bedroom. No matter how much I tried to coax her out, no matter which toys I used, she refused to go past the threshold. Admitting defeat, I turned the walk-in closet into Nina's room. I brought in her food and water bowls and spent the rest of the night turning it into a small paradise for her. Miles agreed to put in a small doggie door so we could keep the kitty litter in the room as well and keep the closet door closed.

"I like Nina's new home," he said as we laid in bed together that night. I did not say anything. I couldn't say anything. December clearly did something to scare Nina to the point where she wouldn't leave the bedroom and I still hadn't found Mew. When I did, I understood why Nina was so upset.

The next day, I went into the basement to do the laundry. There was already a basket of dirty clothes from before our honeymoon so I started with those. I got into the rhythm of reaching down for a handful of clothes and throwing them into the high efficiency front loader, and it wasn't until my fingers grabbed ahold of something stiff that I even looked down. In my hands were a bundle of dirty clothes, but between my pinky and my ring finger was something thin, stiff, and furry. I squealed, dropping everything in my hand back into the basket and took a deep breath fearing the worst. There was no way, right? Slowly, one by one, I peeled away an article of clothing until I uncovered Mew's rigid, dead body. I didn't have the mindset to think, at least she looked peaceful, as I stared down at her unmoving limbs. I couldn't think at all. I didn't even know I was screaming until Miles was grabbing my face begging me to make eye contact with him. "Lana, breathe, honey. Breathe."

Once the screaming stopped, I felt my stomach turn inside out and I thrusted my head into the washer machine as I retched up that morning's breakfast of sausage and eggs. I hurled until my stomach was empty and I was just dry heaving into the washer machine. All the while, Miles sat next to me rubbing my lower back. When I finally drew my head out, I looked to where Mew had been lying on a bed of dirty laundry, to find Miles had covered her back up.

He tucked a strand of hair behind my ear. "Why don't you go upstairs and get cleaned up? I will take care of this down here."

"We have to take her to the vet, Miles," I said in a panic. "I need to know what's wrong. Why this happened. How could this have happened? She's too young. She's barely an adult cat. I don't understand." I started rambling and I could feel my breaths getting caught in my chest. I tried harder and harder to breathe until I was just gasping for air, unable to retain the oxygen.

"Sh, sh, sh," he hushed me, rubbing his thumbs against my cheeks. "Go upstairs. I'll take care of this. Okay? Then we can go to the vet together."

I nodded. Slowly, Miles helped me to my feet and I wobbled up the stairs by myself. I crossed through the dining room, to the staircase. There stood December, leaning against the railing, a smirk on her perfectly sculpted face. In that moment, I knew she had killed my Mew.

Of course, when we took Mew to the vet to be examined, the cause for her death was deemed to be natural causes. But I knew. I knew December had done something to her. Probably poisoned her somehow. Without knowing what she used, I couldn't have the vet test for it. Especially not without raising suspicion from either the vet or Miles.

Miles bought a beautiful bronze cremation urn of a cat with wings sleeping in a woven basket. Mew's new forever home was in that urn, on top of my nightstand, where she could always be close.

I never told Miles I thought December killed Mew. He wouldn't believe me even if I had the proof. December was always going to be her father's little snow angel. Too bad he couldn't see the horns that held up her dimly lit halo. But I could.

November

The school year could not start soon enough. Once it did, it was a nice break for all of us. Between her senior year of high school, picking up a part-time job at a bakery, and time out of the house with friends, December was almost never in the house. It was a blessing to no longer have to pretend that her black hole of a heart wasn't sucking the life out of me. Plus, it gave Miles and me alone time to continue to grow as a married couple.

We fell into a comfortable routine of meeting each other at home after work and settling down at the table to discuss our days over a hot meal, usually provided by the crockpot. After cleaning up, we would migrate to the bedroom where I would take comfort under his warm embrace and fall asleep reading one of my books I had reread several times. Then I would wake in the morning to find the bookmark in place, the book on the nightstand, and a short, but sweet letter from Miles to start off my morning. Maybe it wasn't a spectacular life, but it was the life I had always wanted; a life with Miles.

That is why I didn't know who to even be anymore once I had the sweet taste of my dream life and it turned sour on my tongue. It had seemed to be a day like any other, as the days that change your entire world often do. I had returned home from work before Miles, as usual. And as usual, December was home as well, changing into her work clothes before heading back out the door. I ran into her on my way up to my bedroom, and her way down the stairs. "Oh, hey," she breezily said, as if we were usually friendly to each other.

I gave her a nod which was our usual greeting towards one another.

"You guys were asleep when I came home last night, so I don't know if you saw them, but I brought cookies home for you two. The oatmeal raisins are yours and the double chocolate chip ones are for my Dad."

"Thanks." Oatmeal raisin were my favorite. I thought they would have made a good post-dinner treat. I guess Miles had thought the opposite when he saw them, however. Miles didn't even like oatmeal raisin cookies. I keep wondering, even now, why he would have eaten that cookie. Was he trying to be funny by stealing one of my cookies? I doubt he could have known they would have killed him. I guess I will never know why he chose to eat it.

I spent a good part of the evening getting lost in wonderland as I read *Through The Looking Glass* for maybe the hundredth time. It was pitch black outside before I realized I hadn't heard Miles come home. Normally, he would meet me upstairs where I would typically be lounging in our bed, nose in a book, and he would kiss me with his sweet, rough lips. We would talk about our days, wrapped in each other's embrace. Then, we would eventually succumb to our hunger and cook dinner, together.

It was well beyond dinner time at that point. I checked my phone. No missed calls or text messages. I remember standing up and scaring Nina, who had been asleep on my lap. I remember feeling my heart thump like a jackrabbit against my rib cage as my mind raced so fast that all my thoughts began to blur together. Through my clouding vision, I somehow managed to call Miles on his cell. I held my breath as it rang. When I thought I heard the faintest hint of his phone going off in our mansion of a home, my heart stopped completely. For a brief moment, I thought maybe he had simply gotten out of work late and was on his way up to greet me. I called out his name. The only reply was the persistent ringing of his phone. I can't remember when I started running or screaming his name frantically. All I could think was that I was going to run into him, acting like a maniac and he was going to wonder what the heck was wrong with me. When I followed the sound of his phone to the dining room, I swear everything went silent. There Miles was, sitting on a chair at the table, his eyes open and glossed over. Tears started falling before my mind could even register the scene before me.

I don't remember much after that until the police showed up, spread around our home. I found myself telling the officers everything I remembered without being aware that I was even speaking. Sometime, during the madness, December came home. No one saw it, of course, but when she first stepped inside, she wore an element of pride and her smile was smug. She looked at the police officers like she had just won something. Then her ice-cold eyes met mine and her lips twisted into a disgusted snarl. Her head slowly twisted in the direction of the table and her hands turned to fists at her side. "You dumb bitch!" She squealed as she charged for me. An officer detained her and took her to a separate room to be questioned after she had calmed down.

That was the most genuine emotion I had ever seen December display.

*

Miles' death was ruled out for foul play. They said he simply had a heart attack. I wished it was as simple as that. But I kept replaying the scene of December's reaction repeatedly in my mind. The way she looked at the table before charging at me. Then I thought about Mew's death. I knew in my heart neither of them were accidents, or natural. December had killed them both. Worse, she meant to kill me.

I threw all the cookies away after our house was cleared out. I thought December would want to stay with her aunt as she had when her mother passed away, but she stayed. It got to the point where I didn't trust any of the food in our home. I barely even trusted my soap or shampoo. My only reprieve was getting to leave the house and go to work. There, I could relax slightly. I even piggybacked on a co-worker's gym membership so I could shower outside of the home.

  I would have left. I wanted to leave. But December was unfortunately left in my "care" until she turned eighteen, or unless another family member wanted to take custody of her. I prayed for someone else to take her, but somehow, I was stuck with her. Forced to share a roof with a monster.

December

The weekends were the worst, when I had no escape. Often, I would close myself in the bedroom and solely eat delivery. December usually went to work or went ojut with friends. Even when she wasn't home though, I felt like my life was in danger. Worse, I knew no one would ever believe me.

The first weekend in December, I locked myself in the bedroom and went through Miles' belongings. That Saturday, December's birthday, I went through his old albums and photographs, pulling out pictures and tossing them into the fireplace. December wouldn't care about having any of the photos; she was incapable of caring about anything.

I had gone through most of them when I worked my way up to Frostine's funeral. Who takes pictures at a funeral? I wondered. I thumbed through a few of them before setting them down, realizing our wedding photos were next. I picked up the white album, pressing it against my chest. As if the closer to my heart the album was, the closer to Miles I could be. I thumbed through the pages, a sweet sadness flooding my chest. Miles was so handsome that Spring day. Dressed in a simple black suit and tie. His smile sparkled out of the pictures, making him seem as real as ever. Those crystal blue eyes of his shined like diamonds. How I would have given anything to kiss those beautiful lips one more time. Or to feel his rough hands cupping my chin.

I almost put the album away to abandon the project of the day and try to pretend for a second that my life wasn't completely ruined, when something caught my eye. In the picture of us all together as a "family", there was a woman in the distance staring at December. Something about her was familiar. I had seen her before. In another photograph.

I tossed the wedding album aside and thumbed through the photos of Frostine's funeral again. There she was! Again, and again. She was in almost every photograph. It was clear she didn't belong there. Who was she?

Eventually, I had to put the photos aside and call it quits. How was I going to find someone simply based on a photograph? I called in my order for delivery at the local pizza shop and waited in the living room, pretending to read *Through the Looking Glass*, but never getting further than a couple of paragraphs in. After reading the line, "In another moment down went Alice after it, never once considering how in the world she was to get out again," for the millionth time, the doorbell rang. I sprung up to answer the door, relieved the pizza had finally arrived meaning I could go back and hide in my room pretending I had nothing to fear.

A young, probably twenty-something boy, stood on the doorstep wearing a bright carefree smile. To have innocence again, I thought. He handed me my pizza and the receipt for me to sign. I didn't even look at the total as I tossed it back at him along with thirty dollars. His grin grew as he pocketed the cash. "Thank you. Enjoy your night!"

I returned his smile by forcing the right corner of my mouth up to appear like I wasn't a total bitter recluse. I mumbled something resembling *thanks*, and was about to close the door when I saw her. The same woman from the photographs. She was parked across the street in a midnight blue, or perhaps purple, Mercedes Coupe with her window down. I felt my esophagus walls swell as the anxiety crept up my spine. The boy, oblivious to the fact I had become a statue frozen in disbelief, turned on his heels and jogged to his Torus. The rough start of his engine and the backfire of his exhaust woke me from my spell and I turned on a swivel, slamming the door closed.

Nina weaved between my legs, rubbing against my sweats, meowing at me. "You're right, Nina. I need to stop being afraid."

I went back into the living room, ditching the pizza on the coffee table to peer out the window at the mystery stalker. She sat in her luxury vehicle, earbuds in, doing something on her phone. Panic erupted in my chest once again as my mind raced. Had she bugged our house? I wondered. Why was she stalking us? What was her agenda? Nina peered over the back of the couch with me. She looked out the window, then back at me, and rubbed her face against my cheek. "I needed that, Nina. Thank you."

So, maybe I had gone a little crazy, but I like to think most pet owners can relate. I knew Nina was trying to give me courage. Courage to confront the stranger outside who had been following the family since before I was a part of it. I needed answers.

I took a deep breath and tightened the string around the waist of my sweats. My hair was matted and askew and I couldn't remember the last time I had washed the shirt I was wearing. It was one of Miles' work shirts. I probably wasn't dressed to entertain guests, but if I had gone upstairs to change I would have probably talked myself out of what I was about to do. Another big inhale and I found myself opening the front door. She didn't even seem to notice as she continued to stare at her phone. Bare-footed, I walked down the front steps and out the front gate. I had momentum then and found myself moving faster and faster, only stopping once I was standing on the other side of her rolled down window. I was able to get a good look at her then. Her blonde hair was cut in a bob that aligned well with her sharp cut jawline, which led to her pointed chin. I had to tap on the roof of her Mercedes to get her attention. Once I was up close, I was able to determine the car was in fact blue. Her cat-green eyes looked up at me quickly. She pulled out her left earbud with a smile. "Oh, hi. I'm just waiting for a friend, I'm not breaking any rules, am I?"

She was so slick with her story. Her words dripped with charm and innocence. If I wasn't positive she was the same woman from the photographs, I might have walked away without giving her another thought.

Be brave, I reminded myself. "Who are you?" In my head, those words were supposed to come out harsh and demanding, commanding authority. Instead, they came out like a pathetic whisper.

"Excuse me?" She asked, her voice sweet like a peppermint hot chocolate.

"I know you've been stalking us, okay. You're in our pictures from my wedding. I want to know what you are doing here." I didn't care that I was shaking or that my voice was quaking. I needed to know.

Her smile never faded, but there was a quick change from innocent to knowing. She threw her slender fingers in the air, palms facing forward. "You caught me. I surrender."

"Why are you following us?" I pressed.

"Listen, I don't care about you, okay? I'm after something else. So just go inside and enjoy your takeout and let me do my job." Her dark lashes brushed against her sun-kissed skin as she winked.

I felt anger sliver through my veins. I was not just something people could toss aside and disregard. Again, more forcefully this time, I asked, "Why are you here?"

She looked me up and down, sizing me up. Sighing, she opened her car door and stepped up and out of the vehicle. She was only slightly taller than me, and we were about the same size, except it was clear that she was made of all muscle. I would have never guessed looking at her slender, famine physique, but there was noticeably less body fat on her than there was on me.

"Alright. It's clear you won't let this go." For a brief moment, I thought she would hit me. Knock me out with one punch like in the TV shows and I would wake up in my own bedroom wondering if the exchange was real or not. Instead, she said, "Why don't we go inside and eat your pizza together and I'll explain why you're an idiot?"

That sounded like a much better proposal to me. I nodded and followed the stalker back into the house. I showed her to the living room and went to the kitchen to get us plates. When I went back, the woman had positioned herself on the couch so her body was facing me, but she could still get a clear shot out the window, and Nina was purring on her lap.

Surprised, I exclaimed, "Wow! Nina does not warm up to people. At all."

The woman smiled, "I'm something of an animal whisperer."

I offered her a plate and she took it, opening the pizza box to choose which slice of the chicken and mushroom pizza she would devour first. After picking a slice with a large bubble on the crust, I took a wide slice for myself.

I sat across from her, waiting for the moment she would spill her secrets. Her gaze was fixated out the window, however. It wasn't until she had finished her first slice of pizza that she even acknowledged me. "Not bad. I mean, I've had better, but not bad." She reached for a second slice.

"Who are you?"

She smirked. "More like, what am I." After reading what I am sure was a look of confusion on my face, her thin lips spread into a wider, tighter grin. "Listen, sweetheart. I'm like pest control, okay? And I am here on a job to exterminate the pest in your home."

Instantly, I knew she was talking about December. She could see it too, I thought. She could see that December was evil disguised as an angel. I knew my eyes must have looked wild with the hunger for the truth. I didn't care. Whatever she knew, I needed to know too.

Mouth full, she let out a loud sigh. "Look, there are other things in this world besides humans, right? They can look like humans, speak like humans, but they're not. Got that?"

I nodded, both confused and enticed.

"That girl, your step-daughter, she is not human. She's a pixie."

A pixie? My mind did a quick search of every book I had ever read to conjure up what a pixie was, what one looked like. Popular fairytales painted pixies as fantastical, and small beings that bring joy. True lore painted them as tricksters, sometimes evil. Quickly, my mind pulled up the word *changeling*. Was that what December was, a changeling? My mouth opened, but before I could even make a sound, the woman's hand flew up to stop me.

She continued. Pixies, she said, were emotionless creatures who fed off the despair and pain of others. That was what fueled them. The thought that my fear and despair was *fueling* December infuriated me. While they were cold blooded, they were also beautiful. Even underneath their glamour, which was some sort of magic that made them appear human. Underneath that, however, their features were sharp, their wings were large, fragile, and beautiful, but their teeth were like razors.

Only those gifted with the sight could see through a pixie's glamour. This woman was born with the sight, as most in her family were. Those with the sight had one, extremely important task. To kill pixies.

The source of their power, she told me, was ironically their heart. That was when a cold chill swam down my spine as I realized she had been the one who killed Frostine. When she saw the realization dawn on me, she winked, confirming my suspicions were true.

At first, pixies had to be exterminated because they would kidnap and torture humans, eventually killing them to keep themselves alive. In the beginning, they would swap out human babies with their own for this purpose. Torturing the child and ultimately torturing and killing the families as well. People got smart, they caught on. Eventually, more and more people were born with the sight. So, pixies had to find a different alternative. That's why they started to mate with humans. A child born of pixie and mortal blood were harder to see. It wasn't until they came of age that they could be detected.

Killing Frost wasn't planned. Not really. The woman had just been passing through when she saw her and the unmistakable shimmer of her glamour. She followed her out to the cabin, unaware she was meeting anyone there. "I should have waited," she admitted. "But. . ." A devilish expression danced on her face like flames as she grinned with sin. "The kill was always my favorite part. Creating chaos is a rush. It's like watching a bunch of ants scramble all the while knowing they don't have a chance of survival as you step on them."

Her smile only grew at the thought. I felt my chest tighten, realizing I had let a psychopath into the house. In that moment, fight or flight was kicking in and I was ready to run. But Nina was sound asleep in her lap. I couldn't lose her too. So, I waited for the psycho to tell me the rest of her story.

She stuck around for a while after the kill to check out the cabin. It was clear that no one had been there in a long time. The furniture was covered with plastic sheets that were coated in thick layers of dust. That's when she realized the pixie she killed might have been meeting someone else there. She waited inside the cabin for Frostine's sister to show, watching for her through the front window. Frostine's sister, January, drove up in her Lexus. The woman watched her get out of the Lexus and approach her sister's dead body. Never once did January shout out her sister's name, nor did she run to her to see if she was okay. She calmly walked up to her sister and knelt over her body in the snow. When she saw her sister's heart was missing, she looked up at the cabin, then around herself, knowing a hunter must be nearby. "Damn bitch was smart, though," The woman scowled.

January pulled out her cell phone and dialed the police to report her sister's murder. The woman snuck out the back and hiked back to her vehicle which she had left parked a couple miles up the road.

After killing Frostine, she began to follow the family, determined to figure out how many pixies were involved and prepared to exterminate them all. That's why she was there at the funeral. Why she was at the wedding. It was law, she said, not to kill a pixie before they came of age and transitioned into a full-fledged pixie, marked by their first kill.

"What qualifies as a first kill?" I asked, drawn back into her story. December was becoming of age today and she had already killed. She killed two of the most precious things in my life.

The woman shrugged. "Usually human. Usually with bare hands."

She confirmed that she had been waiting for December to make this first kill. For me to be her first, real kill.

That wasn't going to happen. I couldn't let December fool anyone else. If this woman wasn't going to kill her because of her *rules*, then I would.

That's what I told the woman, standing up, fists clenched at my sides, enraged. She took me in again, a hermit, complete slob, wearing sweats that hadn't been washed in who knew how long. She let out a soft chuckle. "You've got spunk. I'll tell you that." She stood up as well. Dark clouds cast shadows in her eyes. "She's strong. Stronger than you. She will kill you." Her eyes lit back up as the clouds passed. "But don't worry, I'll be here to clean up the mess."

She flashed her pearly white teeth with her cocky smile before heading towards the door. She thanked me for the pizza then retreated to her Mercedes.

I don't know how long I stood in the living room after she left, just trying to digest everything. I felt like I had finally snapped. Maybe she wasn't even here. If she was real, was everything she said true? Was December a pixie? Did pixies exist? Did it matter if what she said was true or not? Either way, I knew December killed Mew and Miles. Either way, I knew it was only a matter of time before she killed me next. This wasn't about fantasy creatures anymore. This was about survival.

*

The large pond in the backyard had iced over for winter. The ice was thick enough for ice-skating. December had already come home from work, or from being out with her friends, or wherever she goes for the entire day. I watched her walk towards the edge of the lake wearing nothing more than a silk, periwinkle, long-sleeved shirt with sleeves that hung off her wrists like the sleeves of a kimono. I watched her from the bedroom window as she flopped her butt onto the ground, only a pair of black leggings separating her skin from the snow. She slipped on the ice-skates and pushed herself off the ground and sprung onto the ice in a fluid motion, propelling herself forward.

I thought of the first time I looked out that bedroom window onto the pond, that lovely autumn day. I thought of Miles and how he smiled while remembering watching his daughter and wife ice-skate. She was beautiful. Her jet-black hair spiraling around her as she twirled on the ice.

Then something inside me really did snap. It was as if there was a tattered rope keeping my sanity in place and, in that moment, the fibers pulled apart with the pressure and my mind unhinged.

I didn't remember grabbing the ice-skates from one of the boxes in the basement. I didn't remember grabbing the hammer from Miles' toolbox, or the knife from the kitchen. I didn't even remember stepping outside. Suddenly, I was there, knife tucked into my boots, and the hammer tucked into the back of my pants. I was on the ice, calling December's name. Her black hair whipped around her head as her ice blue eyes met mine. I think I stopped breathing. My blood sounded like a rushing river as it pumped through my body, fueling it with adrenaline.

Then, a strange calmness washed over me and everything went silent. Our eyes were still locked as I skated towards her, a smile blooming on my face. This was the end. I reached behind my back and lifted the hammer out from its hiding place between my jeans and my back. In one quick, effortless motion I swung the hammer into her ribcage. I felt her ribs give way beneath the steel head. The cracking of her ribs reverberated through the hammer and the sound echoed in my eardrums. She looked confused for a moment, like she didn't know what happened. Then she launched for me. I remembered how the woman said pixies didn't feel anything, it wasn't until that moment I realized she meant physically as well.

Her beautiful, flawless face twisted into an ugly snarl as she flew at me, her hands reaching for my neck. I stumbled backwards, slipping on the ice, and fell between her legs. It wasn't even a conscious thought to use the hammer to shatter her left knee cap, but that's what I did.

She fell onto her left side, confused. I climbed on top of her and she clawed at my face. Her slender fingers wrapped around my neck. I tried to keep my eyes focused as I lifted the hammer above my head and swung it down onto her temple. Her hands went slack and her head fell to the side. I lifted her silk shirt to reveal her white, pump, perky breasts. My face went hot and I felt like a pervert. Not sure if being a pervert would have been worse than what I was about to do. Slipping the knife out from my right boot, I felt the right side of her chest for the broken ribs. For a moment, I hesitated. Would me stabbing her wake her up? Then I figured if she couldn't feel the broken ribs, she probably wouldn't feel me hacking into her chest either.

I held the knife above my head and brought it down with all my force. Once I felt the knife slice through her thick skin into her chest cavity, I started to make a long cut. Her blood oozed thick purple from the punctured skin. That's when I realized she was still breathing. I tried to pretend I was carving into an animal, not December, a young girl, and the daughter of the man I loved. It helped to believe whole-heartedly she was a monster as the woman said. It helped to remember she killed my Mew, my Miles, and she would have killed me. That's what I kept telling myself as I reached into her, feeling for her heart. My fingers wrapped around the organ. It was firm and warm in my hand. It continued to beat against my palm. I realized then I wasn't going to be able to just pull it out. I was going to have to reach back in with the knife to cut the arteries.

I carved the skin of her chest like a door and pulled it open to see where I needed to cut. As I started to disconnect her heart from her body, her eyes flew open and she gasped for air. *Shit*. I had to work faster. She began to squirm. I blindly started stabbing the inside of her chest, trying to hold my position of being straddled over her like trying to stay on a bucking bull. *Fuck it*, I thought. I reached inside her chest with both hands and pulled as hard as I could.

She screamed. Not of pain, but of anger and confusion. As the arteries gave way and her heart was released from her chest, her screams intensified to the extreme of a banshee and then they just stopped. Her heart was in my hand, motionless. Motionless, like its owner. December's black hair was sprawled out around her head in contrast with the white ice. The ice had cracked beneath us from the struggle and her purple blood had filled the cracks around her, branching out like a pair of wings. Her eyes were still open, those icy blues staring up at the night sky blankly as snow floated from above, dancing over her still body. She had never looked more beautiful.

I took her heart upstairs with me and threw it in the fireplace. I watched the flames lick her evil heart clean before devouring it whole.

"And that's when I called the police."

The officers shared a look between them before pushing the notepad and pen in front of me. "Could you please write down your statement for us, Mrs. Snow?"

"Of course."

I could have thrown December's body into the fire and let the snow cover up all evidence of the crime I committed. But I think I just wanted to tell my story. I just wanted someone to know. The media ate it up, painting me as a crazy woman. Maybe I was. I told them a story that no one could collaborate. Especially not the woman, whose name I never knew. A story about mythical creatures and their hunters. A story that would become twisted as being about jealousy instead of friendship, hate instead of love, and I would be the evil one, not her.

Whether I would be sentenced to life in prison or handed the death penalty. I could sleep well knowing I helped rid the world of one evil and I helped spread the word. Because pixies are soulless, cold creatures bent on feeding off our pain. They could be anywhere. They could be anyone. And it is our job to stop them.

Hi y'all. Thank you so much for reading my short story. Loved it?

Hated it? Let me know with a review online.

It would be greatly appreciated.

Many thanks!

-Mercedes Guy Moore

About the Author

Mercedes Guy Moore was married in August 2016 on Folly Beach in South Carolina.

Mercedes is a Mermaid (Well . . . Except for the brief time she was a werewolf) who writes Young Adult Fiction and Fantasy. *What It Took, Daughters of the Ocean Book One*, was a story she weaved together for about seven years. Jumpstarted by her inspiration of Alexz Johnson's song "Voodoo", she self-published Morgan and Emmaline's revised story on September 5, 2016.

She is currently working on a few short stories to be published as ebooks during the next couple of months while *Daughters of the Ocean Book Two* goes under editing and cover design.

Mercedes is attending Southern New Hampshire University online to pursue a degree in creative writing.

For more, follow Mercedes on social media:
[@] authormercedes

Also by Mercedes

What It Took Now Available for Paperback and Ebook on Amazon
and other online retailers.

Morgan never felt like she fit in at school, being half human and half mermaid, and she saw herself as the school's biggest outcast. She led a quiet life with her water nymph guardian, trying to keep her identity a secret in a school of mortals and mythical creatures. Tormented daily by head cheerleader and pixie, Ginger, Morgan finds herself rescued by Leroy, Folly high school's hot new quarterback and vampire, who asks her out on a date. However, Leroy is not all that he seems, and Morgan's life becomes increasingly complicated, confusing and frightening.

Emmaline, a mythical creature herself, moves with her family to Folly and is instantly drawn to Morgan. When the song, "Voodoo" by Emmaline's favorite singer, Alexz Johnson, seems to play on her car stereo every time Morgan is around, she begins to realize that the song's words have a message for her, and she soon discovers that she is destined to save Morgan—but from what, whom or how, she does not know. As the two spend more time together, Emmaline tries to keep her feelings for Morgan separate from her duty to keep Morgan safe, but it soon becomes impossible to deny the intense desires of her heart. Morgan soon discovers the depth of Emmaline's feelings and her undying devotion as she learns

. . . what it took.

(Daughters of the Ocean, Book Two coming soon...)